GIRLS SURVIVE

Raintree is an imprint of Capstone Global Library Limited, a company
incorporated in England and Wales having its registered office at 264 Banbury
Road, Oxford, OX2 7DY – Registered company number: 6695582

www.raintree.co.uk
myorders@raintree.co.uk

Text © Capstone Global Library Limited 2022
The moral rights of the proprietor have been asserted.

Designed by Kayla Rossow
Original illustrations © Capstone Global Library Limited 2022
Originated by Capstone Global Library Ltd
Printed and bound in India

978 1 3982 1489 7

British Library Cataloguing in Publication Data
A full catalogue record for this book is available from the British Library.

Acknowledgements
We would like to thank the following for permission to reproduce photographs:
Shutterstock: Spalnic (paper texture background),
svkv (geometric background)

MOLLY AND THE TWIN TOWERS

A 9/11 Survival Story

by Jessika Fleck

illustrated by Jane Pica

raintree

a Capstone company — publishers for children

CHAPTER ONE

". . . and just as Little Red Riding Hood entered the wood . . ." Papa paused and glanced back at me. He cleared his throat, which meant he was going into an even lower, more menacing voice. ". . . a *wolf* met her."

From the corner of my eye, I saw my little sister, Adi, pull our family cat, Rolo, up next to her. She covered herself and the cat with her quilt.

I smirked and raised my eyebrow at Papa. At twelve, I was getting too old for bedtime stories. These old fairy tales didn't scare me anymore.

I'd moved on to more grown-up books since starting middle school this year.

But my dads considered story time an important tradition. Plus, my little sister lived for it. And since we shared a bedroom . . . I didn't have much choice.

It could be worse, though. At least we read out of the actual Brothers Grimm book. Those stories were pretty strange – definitely creepy.

Across the room, Adeline shivered in her bed. *I* might be too old to be scared, but at seven years old, Adi still got nervous. Even though *Little Red Riding Hood* had been her choice, I knew she'd be keeping me up tonight.

As Papa continued, I forced my eyes to stay open – I couldn't fall asleep yet. I had more important reading to do after he was finished. That's when I read what *I* wanted.

It was as if Papa knew this and read the words extra slowly tonight. When my head nodded backwards, I jumped and sat up taller. From the chair, Dad smiled. I'd been caught.

As Papa continued reading, my mind wandered. My eyes roamed the bedroom I shared with my sister. The old lava lamp we kept on all night made shadows dance against the wall and up onto the ceiling. At certain angles, the light reflected on my snow globe collection.

My collection took up several shelves. Papa brought me one from each new city he visited. As an airline pilot, he visited a lot of different places.

My favourite was the one from Venice, Italy. Inside the small glass globe, a couple sat side by side on a gondola. When I shook the globe, flower petals floated all around them.

Papa read on, ending with the last line, "Red Riding Hood went joyously home, and no one ever did anything to harm her again." With that, he closed the book.

"You know," I said, "I read that in one version the wolf makes Little Red Riding Hood eat her grandmother."

"What?" In her bed, Adi looked horrified. "That's not true, is it?"

She looked at Papa, then Dad for confirmation. Poor Rolo was basically a rag doll in her clutches at this point.

Dad shook his head at me. "Molly, please don't scare your sister."

He had a point. The more scared Adi was, the more likely she was to end up in my bed during the night.

"It's just an old story." I shrugged and gave Adi a soft smile. "Back then they didn't have TV or radio or anything. Books were, like, the only entertainment. Sometimes they got super weird."

I glanced at my bedside table. The book I couldn't wait to dig back into was waiting for me.

"Like *Frankenstein*." I picked it up and showed it to my sister.

Adi cringed at the scary monster on the cover. I placed it facedown on my bed.

"Forget that part. My point is that *Frankenstein* is only a story about a misunderstood monster. *Little Red Riding Hood* is just a story about a girl who meets a mean wolf. But they're just *stories*."

Adi's shoulders softened, and she allowed the cat to move from her lap to the foot of her bed. "But why would Red Riding Hood *eat* her grandmother?"

Just then Gran popped her head into the room. "Did I hear the words 'eat her grandmother' come out of my baby granddaughter's mouth?"

Gran's eyes were wide behind her glasses in exaggerated shock. Adi nodded proudly, but the expression on her face showed I'd freaked her out. I hadn't meant to – not really.

Gran – Papa's mother – came into the room already in her pyjamas, ready for bed. She had lived with us for almost as long as I could remember. She'd moved into our old apartment, temporarily, to help after I was born.

She'd done the same when Adeline came along seven years ago but had ended up staying. With the addition of my sister, we needed a larger apartment, and Manhattan was expensive. Plus, it made sense with busy schedules and Papa travelling so much.

"Listen," Gran said to Adi, "your big sister is full of stories. It's something that'll serve her well one day." She sat next to Adi on her bed. "But for now, you just ignore it and have sweet dreams."

Gran pulled the quilt up under Adi's chin. She tucked it in all around her until she was like a burrito.

Adi smiled happily. We both loved having Gran live with us, me more than anyone. Gran and I were super close. I'd even been named after her.

"Night, Gran," Adi said, barely able to hold her eyes open.

Gran winked at me as she left the room. She'd be back later to say goodnight to me – once my dads had gone to bed. She knew I'd still be reading.

"Finally . . ." I grabbed my copy of Mary Shelley's *Frankenstein*.

Adi's eyes were closed, but just in case, I removed the dust jacket with the picture of Frankenstein's monster.

"Not too late, kiddo," Papa said. "Early flight for me in the morning, so I won't see you." He leaned in and whispered in case Adi hadn't quite drifted off yet. "Keep that goofy sister of yours out of trouble, okay?"

I pressed my lips together and nodded. That was easier said than done. Adi tended to get into a lot of mischief.

Still, I said, "I'll try."

Dad got up from his chair. He gently pulled one of my plaits and kissed me on the forehead. "Sweet dreams, Molly-Moo."

Papa leaned over and gave me a hug. He always smelled of woodsy soap, and his beard tickled my cheek when he said, "Sleep tight. Love you."

"I love you too."

Our dads kissed a sleeping Adi goodnight too. They were almost out the door when I asked, "Wait – where are you flying to tomorrow?"

Papa turned around and came back in. He picked up my newest snow globe, the one from the World Trade Center. We'd taken Dad's parents there when they'd visited from Oklahoma over the summer.

Papa shook it up. "Saint Louis, Missouri."

"With the big arch?"

"That's the one." He looked at me with dark eyes.

Adi had them too. Our dads had used a different surrogate for each of our births. I got Dad's light eyes and dusty hair. Adi got Papa's beautiful darker features and curly hair, which she claimed to hate.

I sat up straighter, opening the thick book to the marked spot. "Papa?"

"Yeah?"

"Don't forget . . ." I didn't have to say exactly what he needed to remember. Papa always knew.

"Never. One Saint Louis snow globe coming your way in a couple of days."

Papa put the globe back and left my room, leaving the door open a crack. I arranged my pillows to make the perfect reading nest. I had just leaned back and set my bookmark to the side when–

"Did you know Mary Shelley first published that book anonymously?" Gran had popped her head back into my bedroom. "People assumed it was her husband who had written it."

"I read that!" I shook my head. "So unfair."

"It was a sexist time. Still is, but it's got better since poor Mary's age." Gran winked. She was full of random facts. "I have to be at the station by seven tomorrow morning for my shift. I'll leave you a surprise in the kitchen, though."

I smiled. Gran's surprises were the best. They could be anything from a piece of chocolate to tickets to a Broadway show.

Gran wasn't your typical grandma. She was an EMT for the New York City Fire Department. She still knitted blankets and cooked and stuff, though, so she said it evened out.

"Night, kid," Gran said. "Don't stay up too late . . . not unless it's worth it."

"I won't." I smiled.

Settling into my bed, I pulled my duvet up to my chin and picked up where I'd left off. I couldn't help the shiver that went up my spine as I read. The lava lamp shadows moving across my wall looked more and more like monstrous creatures by the second. Still, I turned the page and kept reading.

I must have dozed off soon after because I jumped awake at the sound of the floor creaking. I glanced at the clock – midnight.

My book had fallen onto my chest. I picked it up and closed it, then placed it on my bedside table. For a moment, everything was quiet.

Maybe I imagined the noise, I thought.

But then, in the hallway, it sounded again. This time the creak was longer . . . and closer.

I knew *Frankenstein* was just a story, but the only thing I could think about was the monster on the front of my book. His tall, hunched figure would cast a looming shadow across my room. Just like the one the streetlamp cast as it shone against the tall, spindly tree outside my window.

I glanced over at my sister's bed. There was no

movement. She seemed to be sleeping soundly.

I rolled onto my side, curled into my duvet. *There's nothing out there,* I told myself.

But there *was* something out there. It scratched at my door. The hinges groaned as the door opened.

I pulled the duvet clear over my head and squeezed my eyes shut. Quick footsteps padded towards my bed, and my heart leapt into my throat.

"Molly!" a voice hissed from the side of my bed. An annoyed *miaow* followed.

That's all it took for me to realize the culprits. I rolled over and peeked out from under my duvet. Adi, her hair a wild halo of tangles, stood before me. Rolo was held captive in her clutches.

I looked across at Adeline's bed again. My sister's sleeping form was nothing more than a pile of stuffed animals. Her bed had been empty the whole time.

"What are you doing up?" I snapped.

Adi glanced at the door, then back at me. "I got up to get a drink, but then I got scared by a shadow. It looked like a wolf."

I looked at the silhouette stretching from my window to my ceiling. "Shadows can be scary," I admitted. "But it was probably just Rolo. It's okay, I promise."

Adi nodded, squeezing the cat more tightly.

"Can Rolo and I sleep with you tonight?" she asked. Without waiting for an answer, she shoved me over and climbed into my bed.

"Adi, there's no room," I protested.

My sister ignored me and tossed pillow after pillow to the floor. "There. Now there's room." Through the dark, I could see her proud smile.

I sighed. "Fine. *Only* for tonight."

"Okay."

But it wouldn't hold up. It never did. Adi made her way into my bed most nights before Papa would be flying. She was five years younger than me and didn't like the thought of him being gone.

I'd worried about Papa when I was younger too. Now, though, I was so used to him travelling that it didn't bother me anymore. But as much as I reassured Adi that flying was safe and Papa was a good pilot, she still had a hard time.

"Papa will be fine," I said lightly, trying to make

up for being annoyed by her. "He's the best pilot around. He could probably do loop-the-loops if he wanted."

"Yeah?" Adi whispered.

I could see her eyes light up at the idea. "Oh yeah, definitely."

"That'd be cool."

I grabbed the fleece blanket at the foot of my bed and wrapped us up in it. Our room had grown colder since reading. After so many months of summer heat, I couldn't wait for a crisp, autumn-like September. The change would be nice.

I smiled as I drifted back to sleep. I knew there was nothing to worry about. Flying was safe.

CHAPTER TWO

When I woke up what felt like a minute later, my alarm clock was buzzing. From the kitchen, Dad shouted, "Breakfast in ten minutes!"

I sat up to push the snooze button and realized I was alone in the room. Both my sister and the cat had disappeared. Adi had probably got up early to say goodbye to Gran and Papa before they left for work.

I hopped out of bed and opened my window to check the temperature. The minute I did, the sights and sounds of Lower Manhattan hit me.

Cars honked and buses trucked by. Dogs barked and birds chirped. The hum of traffic and chatter of people all mixed together into one low murmur.

The Manhattan skyline greeted me, as it did each morning. The Empire State Building and the World Trade Center were easiest to spot. My school sat just a few blocks away from the tall towers of the World Trade Center.

A breeze wove through the trees and my open window, blowing the yellow curtains like a sail. People seemed to think there was no nature in the city, but that wasn't true. Sometimes you just had to listen a bit harder to hear it.

It was a beautiful September morning. I decided to finally wear the knitted beanie Gran had made for my birthday. Then I threw on my favourite worn jeans, a T-shirt and my trusty high-tops.

"Five minutes!" Dad called.

"Almost ready!"

I ducked into the bathroom and ran a brush through my hair. The beanie would cover the rest.

I rushed to the kitchen. Adi sat on a stool, facing Dad, who poured a cup of coffee for himself across the breakfast bar. Our kitchen wasn't much more than a nook with a fridge and oven, but it was cosy. Printed curtains framed the small window over the sink that housed Gran's mini herb garden.

Dad's idea of a gourmet breakfast was cold cereal and milk, and today he'd gone all out. Five different types of cereal loomed like a cityscape in the middle of the kitchen worktop. A jug of milk stood like a great water tower to their side.

I wasn't a huge cereal fan, but with Papa and Gran gone I would have to make do. I grabbed the box that held the only type I would eat and turned it completely upside down over a bowl.

Nothing.

Well, not exactly nothing. A few sad crumbs and

three perfect, apple-flavoured *O*s dropped into my empty bowl with a quiet clank.

I eyed Adi. Her bowl was overflowing with green and orange *O*s. And she clearly knew what she'd done because the little sneak refused to look at me.

"*Adeline*. You know that's the only one I'll eat!" I said.

"Well, I wanted some too!" Adi shoved a heaped spoonful into her mouth. She chewed, then swallowed. "It's not fair you get them *all*. Besides, it's not like your name's on it."

"Oh, yeah?"

My face turned hot with anger. Maybe it was from the lack of sleep. Adi had tossed and turned all night, rolling herself up like a burrito and stealing all the covers. Maybe it was because all I wanted to eat was one measly bowl of *my* cereal.

Is that too much to ask?

I grabbed the box, turned it to face my sister and

shoved it between her and her spoon, mid-bite. On the front, written in bold, black marker, were the words *Molly's – DO NOT TOUCH*.

Instead of apologizing, Adi rolled her eyes.

I leaned closer, ready to say something I'd probably regret. But before I could, Dad swooped in between us.

"I have a backup!" he announced, setting a light-pink pastry box on the counter. "Well, Gran had a backup. Somehow she always knows, doesn't she?"

Dad opened the box, and inside were two doughnuts – one in the shape of an *M* with chocolate icing and chocolate sprinkles. The other was an *A* with pink icing and rainbow sprinkles.

Gran's surprise, I realized. I forced down the smile that wanted to sneak out. I wasn't finished being annoyed with Adi. Instead, I grabbed the *M* doughnut and went to gather my school things.

Backpack on, I returned to the kitchen to get my

lunch when I remembered Papa's note. He always left a note when he went on a trip.

Sure enough, on the fridge door was a paper held up by fruit-shaped magnets. Papa had drawn his plane and then the loose outlines of New York and Missouri. Hash marks connected one state to the other, marking his path.

A note at the bottom said: *My love soars for you! See you all on Friday! Love, Papa*

I rolled my eyes but smiled. Papa was the king of bad dad jokes.

"You ready, Molly?" Dad asked.

"Yep," I replied.

"Since we're early, I thought we could take the bus part of the way and then walk the last ten minutes or so?" Dad suggested. "It's a nice day outside."

I nodded. "Okay." I liked walking, but with Adi the twenty-minute walk to school took twice the time. We usually took the bus all the way instead.

Dad's plan was a good compromise.

"Plus, you're wearing your hat – might as well get some use out of it." Dad grabbed his keys and wallet. "Adeline, grab your stuff."

As usual, Adi took forever. When she finally returned, she was wearing her favourite rainbow-striped sweater – the one she refused to leave the house without. It had been her baby-blanket – her "woobie" she'd slept with every night.

When Adi had started kindergarten two years ago, she'd decided she was too old for a security blanket. But she also couldn't bear to be without it. That's when Gran turned it into a sweater for her.

"If we hurry, we can still make the bus," Dad said as he helped Adi up. "Piggyback ride?"

She nodded, then climbed onto his back.

We made it to the bus stop without a minute to spare and hopped on. The journey was only fifteen minutes or so. When we got off, we were across the street from the World Trade Center.

I looked straight ahead at the two main towers. They stood like twin pillars, two endless tree trunks reaching up into the sky. I got dizzy every time I looked up at them, but I couldn't help myself.

The towers were beautiful – powerful and delicate at the same time. They looked as though they were made of glass. Like if you threw a stone at a single window, the whole building might splinter and shatter.

But they were also strong. Each glass tower was protected by a series of metal tracks that ran the length of the building, like a lovely birdcage. The tracks helped the towers withstand the gustiest of winds and snowstorms and ice.

Both towers were mostly full of businesses and offices belonging to important financial companies. The New York Stock Exchange was there too.

That stuff didn't really interest me, but I'd

been in the North Tower over the summer, when my grandparents had visited. We'd taken them to Windows on the World – the restaurant near the top. We'd visited the observation deck too.

It was kind of scary being up that high, but mostly it had been beautiful. You could see the entire city from up there.

Dad, Adi and I started walking towards school, a few blocks away from the World Trade Center. Even though Adi and I went to different schools – she was in second grade, and I was in sixth – our schools shared one building.

My part of the school was in the best location. If you looked out the window at the right angle from some of the classrooms you could see the towers.

A cool breeze brushed my cheeks as we walked. Yesterday it had been rainy, hot and humid, but today couldn't be more different. The sky was blue, not a cloud in sight.

Thankfully, Adi moved faster than usual, skipping her way along the pavement. When we made it to the school entrance, the five-minute-warning bell rang.

"You go on, Molly. I'm going to take your sister inside. Have a good day!" Dad said, giving me a hug.

I waved goodbye to Adi. When I walked around the corner to the entrance of my school, I nearly slammed into my best friend, Zach.

"Molly!" Zach exclaimed. A huge grin stretched across his face. Zach was always way too happy about being at school. "Walk much?" He giggle-snorted, his signature laugh.

"Yeah, yeah . . ." I rolled my eyes playfully. Zach and I had been best friends since about second grade. I wasn't offended by him giving me a hard time.

Before I could say more, the final bell rang. I followed Zach's familiar outfit – blue baseball cap, T-shirt and jeans – down the corridor. We rushed into our classroom just before Ms Hayden closed the door.

Our teacher took the register while the morning announcements played over the intercom. I got lost in the beautiful day outside, distracting myself counting how many people were walking their dogs.

I'd just counted dog number five – a scruffy black-and-white puppy that looked like a teddy bear – when the strangest thing happened. As if they'd rehearsed it, everyone in the street stopped at the same exact time. They literally halted mid-step.

Then they all looked up.

Before I could work out why, a huge *boom* erupted outside. It almost sounded fake, as if I was in a cinema and the surround sound was turned all the way up. But this was real life.

The noise shook our entire school like a humongous, angry clap of thunder. The glass in the window next to me shuddered. I jumped in my seat and clapped my hands over my ears.

For a moment, everyone was still. Then the

entire class rushed towards the windows as hazy smoke filled the view.

On the street, the same people who, moments earlier, had been frozen in place were now running.

CHAPTER THREE

Riverfront Middle School
Lower Manhattan
11 September 2001
8.50 a.m.

The scene outside was like nothing I had ever seen. People in the city tended to move quickly – everyone was always late for something – but this was mass confusion. It was as if no one knew where to go or what to do, but everyone was trying to get somewhere else, and fast.

My heart raced in my chest. *What is going on?*

Outside, the smoke grew thicker.

"What do you think it is?" Zach asked.

I assumed he was talking to me, even though he was still looking out of the window.

"I have no idea," I replied. "But it can't be good."

We all talked at once, everyone asking questions. Finally, Ms Hayden got our attention.

"Everyone, try to stay calm," she said. "I'm sure everything is all right. I'm going to step out into the corridor to see if there's any information. Please stay in your seats and find something quiet to do."

Yeah right, I thought. *That's like asking Adi to sit still with a pile of puppies in front of her.*

The minute Ms Hayden left, everyone went back to chattering and speculating. There were theories from a fire to a bomb to a car accident.

I didn't think it had been a car accident – the people on the street had all looked up at the sky. But suddenly anything seemed possible. And none of it made the pit in my stomach feel any better.

Part of me wanted to speculate too, but it was as if I was frozen. Just like those people outside my window had been. Only I wasn't staring up at the sky. Instead, I was biting my fingernails. Worried. Afraid.

And if I was worried, how must Adi feel? What was happening in her classroom? I was surrounded by sixth graders who could barely keep calm. I couldn't imagine how a load of six- and seven-year-olds must be reacting.

Just then, Ms Hayden came back into the classroom. Before she could say anything, the ding that signalled an announcement sounded over the loudspeaker. Everyone went still.

The principal's voice came through the speaker: "Teachers and students, there is a large fire near the top of one of the World Trade Center towers. There is no need to worry or panic. However, we will be calling your parents to come and pick you up from school. In the meantime, your teachers will instruct you to move to either the gym or the cafeteria. Please be orderly, quiet and calm."

A fire? I thought. *At the top of the tower?*
If that was supposed to make me feel better, it
didn't. *Maybe it's the restaurant? Fires start in*
restaurants all the time, right?

Still . . . something didn't feel right.

We left the classroom and made our way down
the corridor in single file. I couldn't help but notice
that all the adults looked worried. It was as if they
were talking to one another without using words.
Based on their expressions, the conversations didn't
seem good.

As we walked, I overheard a couple of parent
volunteers talking.

"The fire's enormous," one whispered.
"It's engulfed several floors of the tower."

"I heard a plane crashed into it," the other one
replied.

The words cut through me like a freezing gust
of wind.

I leaned closer to Zach, who was walking right in front of me. "Did you hear that?" I whispered.

He glanced back over his shoulder. "A plane? There's no way." But his voice wasn't very convincing.

Zach had to be right. How could that even happen? I'd heard stories of planes crashing in fog and other bad weather, but the sky had been completely clear on our walk this morning.

I shook my head in disbelief. *No, it isn't possible,* I told myself. *Those parents must have heard wrong.*

The corridors were growing more crowded now. More people, kids and adults, began talking. Things quickly got out of hand.

There was more chatter about a plane hitting the tower – someone said it was a small prop plane. Papa had taken us up in one of those last spring. Others were saying it was a passenger jet, an idea I refused to consider. If that was the case, then Papa . . .

No. It was unimaginable. Passenger jets didn't crash into buildings.

My thoughts went to Adi. She was already worried about Papa flying. What if she was stuck in a crowded corridor too? What if she overheard adults talking about a plane crashing into one of the towers?

I knew my sister. She might not show her fear – not at first, anyway. But she would definitely act on it. Whether the plane rumour was true or not, I had to get to Adi before she heard about it from someone else.

I continued down the corridor, surrounded on all sides. One thing about the chatter around me was consistent – the fire raging at the top of the North Tower had grown. Flames were billowing up onto the top of the building.

The strong, delicate glass building.

How can this be happening? I thought.

Sirens sounded in the distance, and I instantly thought of Gran. Her station was nearby and would probably be one of the first to respond to the fire.

My heart sank. Gran dealt with a lot of emergencies as an EMT, but imagining her going into that tall tower . . . my head ached with worry.

As more people squeezed into the small corridors, some kids began to push. The single-file lines we'd formed were quickly forgotten. They were replaced with shoving and shouting. Teachers tried to gain control by raising their voices.

Zach was further ahead of me now. He glanced back and our eyes met. There were too many people between us for me to catch up. As the corridor narrowed and the kids closed in on me, it got harder to breathe. My throat closed, and my head went dizzy.

I had to get out of here.

Looking over the sea of kids, I spotted the corridor back to my classroom. It led in the opposite direction and was mostly empty.

"Zach!" I called. I stood on my toes to catch a glimpse of my friend. "Zachary!"

When he turned and made eye contact, I pointed to the corridor. Then I started shoving my way towards it.

Squeezing through the crowd was like swimming against a current. I pictured Adi, small and worried, doing the same thing in her school and felt dizzy again.

Stop it, I told myself. *That's not helping.*

Imagining my little sister crying and confused wasn't going to get me to her any faster. Picking up my pace would.

When I finally made it to the empty corridor, relief washed over me. I could breathe again.

Zach rounded the corner a minute later. He had taken off his hat, and his dark hair was a shaggy mess.

I was still out of breath but managed to say, "I have to get to Adi."

Zach looked at the empty corridor before us, then back towards the loud, crowded gym entrance. "Do you think we can?" he asked. "Won't the teachers stop us? Do you think we can even get to her side of the building?"

"I have to at least try." I started walking further away from the commotion around the corner. "You know how scared Adi gets when our dad flies. Zach, if she hears about the–"

"–plane," he finished for me. "I know."

I could only nod. I started walking more quickly, searching for the best way out.

"I'm sure she's fine," Zach said, trying to reassure me.

I glanced back at him. He must have seen the worry on my face, despite me trying to hide it. All he said was a confident, "We'll find her."

"Thanks," I said, swallowing back my fear. I knew Zach cared for Adi like she was his little sister too.

Zach and I linked arms and took a hard right. I pulled him down a corridor that led to an exit. I kept waiting for a teacher or parent to stop us, but no one did.

It was too chaotic. Inside, everyone was rushing towards the back of the building and into the gym. Outside, people on the street were frantically running past the windows.

I spotted the side door. It led outside onto West Street and then to a path that linked the elementary school to our side of the building.

I started to pull Zach towards it when . . .

BOOM!

CHAPTER FOUR

Riverfront Middle School
Lower Manhattan
11 September 2001
9.02 a.m.

A louder, crashing explosion sounded from outside. This one was so intense that I felt it in my chest. The blast made my ribs rattle, and the sound echoed within me.

The shock of it threw me off balance. I stumbled forward into the door, my arm still locked with Zach's.

"What was that?" I gasped.

"Another plane?" Zach asked. He squinted out of the nearest window, but it was impossible to know what was happening a hundred storeys above.

"No. It can't be," I said.

I couldn't believe one plane had hit, let alone two. It had to be something else. Had the fire caused an explosion?

But that noise . . . It was eerily similar to the crushing boom we'd heard in the classroom. And if people were right about the first plane . . .

My mouth went dry, and my eyes stung. I was frozen with fear. At the same time, I was so terrified that I itched to flee.

When I glanced down the corridor, teachers were hurriedly ushering kids into the gym. The intercom rang, and the principal's voice came over the speaker again. Her voice was shaky, but the directions were firm.

"Attention, please. We have been instructed to evacuate the entire school. Teachers are to take all students to the emergency location behind the school down by the waterfront. *Immediately.*

In order to stay safe, please remain orderly, quiet and calm."

For fire drills, we normally went to the public baseball field next to our school. But the baseball field wasn't far from the World Trade Center. If we couldn't go to the usual safe place, I quickly realized, things must not be safe out there at all.

"Let's get going," I said to Zach. I tried to push everything to the background. I had to focus on finding my sister.

We walked out the door and onto West Street. But nothing could have prepared me for the scene that unfolded before us.

It was deafeningly loud but also incredibly still at the same time. A horrible yellow-grey haze filled the air, clinging to everything. It was as if the entire Lower West Side was trapped inside a foggy cloud.

People ran this way and that, but mostly they seemed to be running *away*.

I looked up . . . and immediately regretted it.

Fire and smoke raged and billowed out of the top portion of the North Tower. The South Tower, now also on fire, was quickly catching up. Debris rained down as if the sky was falling.

My throat closed up from fear and shock. I felt close – too close. The intense heat radiating off the towers pushed against my face like a sunburn.

Sirens blared. Emergency vehicles drove on the pavements to get through the crowds. People with injuries, their clothes covered in ash and dust, sat on the pavements. Others stumbled down the street as emergency workers stepped into action.

I looked back up at the buildings, stunned. Someone passing by shouted, "It was a passenger jet . . . two of them!"

I opened my mouth to ask how they knew that – how that could be possible – but the person was already gone.

I didn't want to believe it. I held on to my doubt. I wouldn't accept it until I knew. Because passenger jets, like the ones Papa flew, didn't just crash into buildings.

Then two men quickly walked past. "One plane might be an accident," one said, "but two?"

"That's no accident," the other man agreed.

No accident? I thought. *How could it not be an accident?* Planes didn't crash into buildings. Not on purpose.

Their comments didn't make sense, but the men were gone before I could ask what they'd meant.

I glanced over at Zach. He had his head tilted upwards, staring in horror at the towers. "Zach?"

"Yeah?"

"Let's find Adi."

I forced my legs to walk towards Adi's side of the school. I wasn't sure if it was the smoke or fear, but my chest cramped. I felt sick to my stomach.

I have to find my sister.

I'd only gone a few steps when I realized Zach wasn't with me. I turned back and saw him still standing there, eyes focused on the buildings. He hadn't moved an inch.

I grabbed his hand. "Come on!"

When we reached the elementary school entrance, kids and adults were piling out the door and onto the street. I pushed against the flow of people, trying to squeeze my way inside the building.

A couple of adults tried to stop us. One woman, probably a teacher, motioned us away with her hands. "We have to evacuate!"

But there were so many people pushing, shoving, running – trying to get far from the smoke and heat. The teacher quickly moved on. She wanted to be away from here. Everyone did.

I wanted that too. But not without Adi.

Zach and I ran towards my sister's classroom. I'd never seen the school so empty. Even at the end of the day, there were always some kids and teachers or the maintenance crew walking about.

Now there was no one. Only Zach and me and the haze that had sneaked its way in with us.

"Adeline!" I shouted, racing down the corridor.

"Adi! Where are you?" Zach shouted in another direction.

I quickly spotted the door to Adi's classroom. It was covered in construction-paper cutouts of rain clouds and sunshine and flowers. Each flower had a child's name on it. Adi's was bright orange. She'd drawn a face with whiskers and cat ears.

We pushed the door open.

Nothing.

Not one child or teacher.

What was usually a room full of rambunctious second graders was eerily empty and silent.

Panic threatened to overtake me. The creepiness of the empty school combined with horrible scenes unfolding just outside were too much. I had to get to my sister and get us out of there – fast.

"We're too late," I said, still searching the empty space. "She must have evacuated with the others." I hoped that was true.

Zach placed his hand on my shoulder. "That's a good thing," he said. "That means she got out. We'll find her. I know she's safe."

But as I turned to leave, something caught my eye. Adi's rainbow-striped sweater hung all by itself on a hook next to the door.

She would never have left school without it.

Adi was here somewhere. And it was up to me to find her.

CHAPTER **FIVE**

Riverfront Elementary School
Lower Manhattan
11 September 2001
9.30 a.m.

"I think Adi's still in the school," I said.
I quickly yanked the sweater off the hook and
dashed out of the classroom.

Zach was right behind me. "Where do you
think she is?"

"I'm not sure," I admitted. "But you know
Adi doesn't go anywhere without this sweater."

I headed towards the back of the school. Adi
could have gone back to the gym.

*That's probably where they were headed before
the evacuation,* I thought.

But as I raced down the corridor, I passed a door plastered with kids' paintings and it hit me – the art room.

I skidded to a stop. Adi loved art. She talked about the space all the time. There was a loft where she sat on a beanbag and drew in her sketchbook. She'd even tried to re-create the space in our bedroom with my desk, a couple of chairs and borrowed sofa cushions.

I'd stopped so fast that Zachary nearly slammed into my back. "What's wrong?" he asked.

"The art room." I turned and pushed the door open. Inside, it was empty and dark.

Zach started searching the supply cupboards. I climbed the stairs to the loft. I prayed I would find my sister sitting safely among the cushions and chairs. But when I reached the top, the loft was empty.

My stomach dropped with disappointment.

"She's not up here," I called down to Zach.

"No luck down here either."

I started back down the stairs, but a pile of pillows in the corner caught my eye. It was pretty big – big enough to hide in.

I climbed back up, walked to the pile of pillows, and removed a couple. Sure enough, Adi lay there, hidden.

"Adi!" I grabbed my sister and pulled her to her feet. "Thank goodness! Zach, I found her!"

"Mollyyyy?" Adi blinked up at me. Her hair was no longer in the plaits from this morning. Now she had a mess of dark curls framing her face. She also had a fresh hole in the left knee of her jeans. "I thought I heard someone, but I was too scared to come out."

I pulled her into a tight hug. "What are you doing in here all alone?" I said into her hair. "I was so worried!"

Adi looked up at me. "I followed my class to the gym, but I remembered I forgot my sweater. I had to go and get it. But then they said we had to leave the school and everyone started running. There were so many people, and I tripped and fell and tore my jeans." She sniffled. "I got scared, so I hid in here."

"No one stopped you from leaving your class?"

Adi shook her head. "I was sneaky. Plus, it was really loud and crazy."

"Yeah, our side of school was like that too," I said. "We need to get down to the riv–"

Before I could finish, fire alarms started blaring. Adi covered her ears.

"It's going to be okay!" I shouted. I looked down to where Zachary stood waiting below. "Let's get out of here!"

He nodded, and I helped Adi down the stairs. Together, the three of us started down the corridor and out the back exit.

Outside, the scene had worsened. Some people were pushing their way through the crowd. Some stared blankly at the sky. Others cried as if they weren't sure what else to do.

I wasn't sure either. I wanted to do each of those things – run and cry and scream and keep watching – all at once.

A full block away from the towers, the heat of the fires was strong. And the flames were growing. The smoke was blackening.

Many had stopped and were simply watching. Some talked to one another. One man had a radio on full volume. A newscaster's voice tried to make sense of what was happening.

". . . all of the world watches and waits, wondering how this great tragedy will unfold. How two planes could crash into one of Manhattan's most renowned landmarks is beyond shocking. Our hearts are with the people of New York City this morning. . . ."

Without deciding it, the three of us stopped and listened.

". . . terrorist groups are claiming responsibility for the attack. It is now assumed that this was no accident. America has been attacked. If you are in Manhattan, all agencies recommend you seek shelter."

There was a pause, then . . .

"This just in . . . my lord . . . excuse me. . . . I-I'm getting reports that another passenger plane has crashed into the Pentagon building in Washington, D.C. I repeat . . ."

"Planes?" Adeline looked up at me, panic in her eyes. "Papa's flying today. Is it Papa's plane?"

I took her by both her hands. "No. Absolutely not. Papa's plane took off very early this morning. He's already in Saint Louis by now, Adi."

At least, that's what I hoped. Because if I was being honest, I didn't know for sure. Not really. Planes got delayed all the time.

At least Adi hadn't realized that Gran could be in danger too. If her fire station had been one of the first to respond, she could be in the towers right now.

Our grandmother was strong and tough and smart, but she was getting older. I knew Dad and Papa had been urging her to retire.

I imagined Gran searching for the injured. Struggling to scale the stairways of the World Trade Center. Surrounded by smoke.

My chest ached and I forced a deep breath. I couldn't afford to panic right now. We had to get out of here first.

Papa and Gran have to be okay, I told myself.

But the pit in my stomach told me that might not be true.

Just then the radio cut back in: "Planes are being rerouted. All flights are grounded. We have no idea how many other jets could be hijacked."

CHAPTER SIX

Hijacked? I didn't know what that meant. But I knew that planes did not run into buildings. Not with experienced pilots.

And if people were worried it could happen again, what did that mean? Could someone have forced the pilots to–

No, I told myself. I couldn't think about that right now. Papa would never.

That knot that had been getting lodged in my throat all morning took hold again. Papa was safe. He had to be.

We had to get moving. The world didn't make sense. I didn't know what else could happen – what else could be coming.

Could more planes be set to hit other buildings around us? I worried.

"We have to get home," I said. It seemed like the safest place to be.

"What about my apartment?" Zach asked. "It's closer."

I looked in the direction of Zach's apartment in Battery Park City – the same direction as the burning towers. All I saw was smoke and chaos. Workers were blocking off streets.

Zach realized it too. He pulled his baseball cap from his back pocket and stuck it on his head as if he were donning a uniform.

"Your place, it is," he said.

Zach, Adi and I took off, weaving in and out of people and abandoned cars. We weren't the only ones to flee. Most people moved in our same direction – away.

We were a few blocks from the towers now, but it still smelled like the world was on fire. And not the good kind of fire, like a fireplace in the winter. This was a harsh, chemical smell. It was unnatural. My chest burned when I breathed in.

We came up on the street that led to the ferries. The riverfront was packed with people. The lines for ferries branched off in several directions.

I skidded to a stop. Adi was holding tightly onto my hand and jerked to a halt too. We were on a familiar corner, but nothing looked like what I was used to.

For a moment, I didn't know what to do. Any street we took could be filled with crowds or blocked off. We could be met with speeding fire trucks or ambulances.

"This way!" I pointed to the street we'd normally take. If it was crowded, at least it would be our usual route. "Come on!"

We passed a group of emergency workers on foot, followed by sirens and several ambulances. They were all moving towards the towers.

My thoughts went back to Gran. *What time did she say her shift was today? Seven o'clock? Could she be there right now, inside the building, climbing all those stairs?*

It was almost too much to consider.

More sirens blared. Living in the city, sirens were a common noise. I heard them all the time, day and night.

But today, everything was amplified. It felt like there were a hundred times more sirens than normal. And maybe there were.

Once we reached the other side of the short alleyway, I stopped and turned in a full circle. I couldn't catch my breath. The panic of everything – the fires, the planes, Papa, Gran – all came crumbling down on top of me.

"I don't know what to do, Zach," I said. "I don't know where to go."

Zach looked as hopeless as I felt. But still, he said, "We have to keep moving. We don't know if it's safe here."

The moment we turned left, following the sign to North End Avenue, a sound like nothing I'd ever heard before seized the air. It was a deafening thunderclap followed by the roar of a thousand train engines.

I stopped and turned back towards the monstrous noise. The image before me was pure horror.

A plume of dust and smoke rose up out of the city like an erupted volcano. The black cloud was as high as the South Tower was tall.

The smoke and debris began where the tower stood and tumbled forward. It was like a large wave, quickly engulfing everything in its path, threatening to wash us all away.

There was exactly zero time to think about anything except getting as far away as possible.

CHAPTER SEVEN

Lower Manhattan
11 September 2001
10.00 a.m.

Everyone around us ran. I pulled Adi along with me. I refused to loosen my grip on her hand.

At some point, I noticed my right shoe was untied and loose. Then, several quick paces later, it was gone. I was now running around the city in a black-and-white polka-dot sock. Gran would lose it if she knew.

My chest dipped at the thought of Gran. What if she had been in or near the towers just now?

Will I ever get to talk to her again? I just want to know she and Papa are safe.

I pushed my legs to move even faster, pulling Adi with me. Zachary worked to keep up with us. Finally, my legs could no longer move. I'd run several blocks and my chest burned and ached. I had to stop.

Zach caught up to me and hunched over, panting, hands resting on his knees. When he looked up, horror filled his eyes.

I followed his gaze, looking back in the direction from which we'd run. I looked at where the tower stood . . . except there was no tower.

The South Tower, a larger-than-life skyscraper, was gone. It had fallen like a house of cards. What was once something grand, a beacon I'd come to know and recognize, was now . . . nothing. There was only smoke and sky.

A sound that I didn't recognize left my body. A sort of gasp mixed with a sob. Looking around me, everyone wore the same expression – sadness, exhaustion, fear.

Smoke and dust still filled the air. Fire raged on from the top of the North Tower – now a lone pillar.

I realized with horror that I was alone too – in the chaos, I had somehow lost track of Adi. She wasn't with me.

"Adeline!" I screamed.

I stood, helpless and frozen. I'd sworn I wouldn't let go of her hand. I didn't remember letting go.

Others around us called for the names of people they'd been separated from. The monstrous dust cloud was now a haze. It hung in the air like a dark fog.

"Adeline Eugenia!" I shouted again. I used her full name, the way Papa and Dad did when they wanted to get her attention.

Zach followed my lead, calling out her name in different directions.

I tried to think clearly, but it was impossible.
I wasn't sure where exactly to go.

Should I head back towards the towers? Should I stay put? Should I work my way to our house and hope Adi did the same? What if I never find her? What if she's hurt or lost or can't breathe from all the smoke?

I turned in a circle, glancing from face to face, street corner to street corner, and building to building. I didn't know when I started crying, but tears were streaming down my cheeks.

"Molly?"

The voice was so small compared to the background noise and the blood rushing to my ears. I almost didn't believe I'd heard it.

But when I glanced down, there she was. My little sister was standing in front of me and holding my missing shoe.

I couldn't believe it.

I dropped to my knees, scooped her into a hug, and sobbed into her hair. "Adi, where did you go?" I couldn't keep the fear out of my voice. "I was so worried!"

Adi was crying now too. "I was running and running and I couldn't find you, and I got so scared and then I found your shoe. I knew you couldn't be too far away."

I knelt there, clutching my sister and crying, until I felt a gentle pat on my back. I looked up to see Zach. He had tears in his eyes too.

"We should keep moving," Zach said. Adi and I nodded.

I slipped my shoe back on. Moving in what felt like slow motion, we started making our way to our house, moving north, further into Tribeca.

It was comforting but also strange. We were still relatively close to the fires and sirens. People stood on their porches and roofs in stunned disbelief.

"Why didn't Dad come and get us from school?" Adi asked.

I glanced down at her. "He probably didn't have time," I replied. "I mean, I bet it wasn't long after parents were called that they started closing off roads. Even if Dad ran the whole way, he'd have been stopped by crowds and fire trucks and who knows what else."

"Yeah . . . ," she said.

"He tried to get to us," I said. "I know he did. We'll find him at home. And if he's not there, I'm sure he'll come home soon to find us."

Of course, I *wasn't* sure. But worrying about Papa and Gran was already too much to handle. I could not add Dad to the list. He had to be safe.

I didn't have any more time to dwell on the promises I was making because just then a horrible sound rang through Lower Manhattan. My stomach clenched with dread. It was a sound I'd already heard once this morning. This time it was further off. Not so close it seized my breath, but close enough it sent a wave of terror throughout my body.

We all stopped walking and turned to look back. Like a sandcastle being taken down by the tide, the North Tower tumbled into nothing.

The sound of the collapsing building was like a hundred trains racing towards us. Now both Twin Towers had fallen. There was a gaping, smoking hole in the New York City skyline.

And once again, the smoke and dust rushed towards us.

CHAPTER EIGHT

The three of us linked hands and ran as fast as we could while still staying side-by-side. We would not be separated again.

The haze reached us quickly, but we were further away than when the first tower fell. We ran for blocks. Eventually our pace slowed to a jog, then a walk. Our legs were tired. Our lungs burned.

"Finally," I breathed as we reached our neighbourhood.

I stopped and looked back towards where the towers stood – or had stood. It was as if someone had put together a puzzle of a New York cityscape, but two very important pieces were missing.

I couldn't begin to think about the people who'd been inside those buildings. Hundreds and hundreds of people went in and out every day. I often watched them from my classroom window.

Were they able to get out? Had there been enough time? Had Gran . . .

Before I could finish the thought, tears filled my eyes and blurred my vision. My throat tightened with emotion.

Both towers had now fallen. If Gran had been near the World Trade Center, much less inside one of the buildings . . .

"Molly?" Adi said.

I wiped my eyes with my sleeve and swallowed back my tears. It was hard to be strong for my little sister right now, but I had to try.

"Yeah?" I gazed down at her.

"How much longer do we have to walk?"
she asked.

"Almost there," I promised.

As we made our way down the street, the
only neighbourhood I'd ever known suddenly felt
foreign. Everything was one step off.

The traffic noise was strange. Instead of
buses running and taxis and cars honking, it was
mostly silent. Those sounds had been replaced by
helicopters and military jets overhead. Behind that
was the constant wail of sirens and alarms.

Even our neighbours didn't quite look like
themselves. Many sat on their porches. Some stood
in the streets. No one seemed to know what to do.

"Are you kids all right?" a woman called to us.
"Cell service is completely out. Do you need to
borrow our house phone?"

"That's okay," I answered. "We're almost
home."

She looked concerned but only nodded. Then she went back to staring at where the World Trade Center had stood.

The closer we got to home, the quicker my pace became. I exhaled in relief when I spotted our apartment building, but then I realized something. Just because we were home didn't mean things were okay.

If today had taught me anything, it was that nothing was safe. Things had shifted since we'd left for school. It was almost impossible to believe it was even the same day.

I just hoped Dad was home.

I still held Adi's hand tightly, but I shoved my free hand in my pocket and crossed my fingers. It was then, as I looked down at my jeans, that I realized my clothes were covered in dust.

I looked at Adi. Her hair was covered in white powder. So was Zach's baseball cap. We

looked like we'd been caught in an unseasonable
snowstorm.

I stopped and looked up at the sky. It was
snowing. Except it wasn't snow – it was ash, falling
from the sky.

I'd heard of this happening when volcanoes
erupted. But I'd never imagined it would happen
in my neighbourhood. In Manhattan.

"Oh . . . ," Adeline said. She pointed to the row of buildings that dotted our street. Everything from cars to lawns to roofs had a sad, ashy luster.

The sight brought fresh tears to my eyes. *Will things ever go back to the way they were before today?* I wondered. *Will I always see ash coating my neighbourhood? Even once the ash is long gone?*

The three of us slowly climbed the steps leading to our building. There, I turned and stole one last look at the skyline. Those two great towers that greeted us each morning were gone. Only a dark cloud of smoke remained.

I didn't want to think it, let alone have it be true, but I knew . . . if the buildings were gone, chances were many of the people who'd been inside them were gone too.

And what if one of those people was Papa? Or Gran?

A scratchy lump lodged in my throat.

Before I opened our apartment door, I took a deep breath. I made a silent plea – a wish or a prayer. I hoped that Dad and Gran were inside. That Papa was safe in Saint Louis.

But when I pushed the door open, the apartment was dark. Quiet.

"Gran?" I called. "Dad? Hello?"

No one answered. Not even Rolo came out to greet us.

My heart raced. The events of the morning were finally catching up to me. After so much worrying and running and horror, after watching the Twin Towers fall, coming home to a dark, empty house threatened to push me over the edge.

Everything felt as if it was floating around me as I turned in a circle. Again, I called out, "Dad? Are you here? Gran?" My voice shook.

But no one answered. We were alone.

CHAPTER NINE

Molly's apartment
Tribeca, New York City
11 September 2001
10.55 a.m.

"Rolo!" Adeline shouted from our room.
"There you are!"

My sister's voice snapped me back into action.
I ran to the phone mounted on the kitchen wall.
My fingers were numb as I dialled Dad's mobile. It
rang once, then stopped.

I tried again.

Same thing.

"Any luck?" Zach asked. He came into the
kitchen and poured a glass of water for himself,
then two more for Adi and me.

"No. That lady was right. Cell service must be down." I tried again, one last time, but the call dropped for a third time.

I handed the phone to Zach. "Do you want to try calling your house phone?" I asked.

He nodded and dialled, then shook his head. "Busy," he said.

Zach tried several more times with no luck. Finally, on the fifth or sixth attempt, his eyes lit up.

"Mum?" he said. Emotion made his voice break.

I left to give him some privacy. Walking into the living room, I found Adeline cradling Rolo.

"Where was he?" I asked.

"Hiding underneath my bed. He was so scared, Molly." She pulled him closer. "Everything's gonna be okay, Rolo. I'm here now. . . ."

I hoped my sister was right, but I had no way of knowing if that was true. Just then, the sound of someone running up the steps echoed through the apartment. A moment later, the front door burst open.

"Molly? Adeline?"

Dad.

Before I could say his name, Dad ran into the living room and scooped us into his arms. Rolo managed to get away, much to his delight.

"I was so worried . . . ," Dad said.

"Is Papa–" I started to say. I couldn't even finish the sentence.

Dad pulled back, and I saw the tears in his eyes – tears of relief. "It was *not* one of Papa's planes," he said. "He's safe in Saint Louis. They've grounded all flights . . . just to be careful."

"And Gran?" I asked.

"Gran's safe too," Dad said. "She's working very hard near the World Trade Center. I was able to check in with the station about ten minutes ago.

I had to stop and use a pay phone because cell service is down."

I literally fell into his arms, relief washing over me.

"I've been trying to get to you two all morning," Dad said, squeezing us more tightly.

"That's what Molly said!" Adi patted my shoulder with her small hand.

Dad looked me in the eyes. "She was right." He pulled back a bit to get a better look at us. We were in much worse shape than he was, but he too wore the same dusting of ash. "And she got the two of you home safely, just like I knew she would."

"Three of us, actually," I said just as Zach walked in from the kitchen. He waved at my dad.

"Zach, are you okay? Did you call your mum?"

"Yes . . . to both. She's on her way."

Again, Dad took a long look at us. "You three have been through a lot this morning."

We all nodded.

"Can you tell me about it?" Dad asked.

I looked from Zach to Adi, and they nodded.

"Okay," I said.

My dad spread out a blanket, and we all piled onto the sofa. It was exhausting, but we took turns recounting the past few hours.

When we finished, there was a moment of silence. No one said a word.

"My goodness," Dad finally said. "What a long, scary morning. I'm so glad you had each other. You were all so brave."

Not too long after, Zach's mum arrived. When she came into our apartment, there were tears running down her cheeks.

"I was so worried," she whispered, wrapping Zach up into a tight hug.

Zach didn't seem embarrassed by his mum's affection. He hugged her right back.

After they'd left, Adi and I went to take showers. It took a long time to get all the dirt and dust out of my hair, but eventually the water ran clear.

When I came back into the living room, Dad was watching the TV on mute. A wet-haired Adi was asleep on the sofa next to him. Rolo lay curled up at her feet.

"Today was a lot, huh, Molly?" Dad said.

I nodded and finally allowed the tears to fall freely. Dad held out his arms, and I joined him on the sofa, squeezing in next to him. He wrapped his arm around me and covered me up in one of Gran's crocheted blankets.

I settled into the embrace. Right now, it was exactly what I needed.

We sat there for a long time in silence. Dad didn't ask me any questions, and I was thankful for that.

Finally, Dad said, "I spoke to Gran while you were in the shower."

It was like I could finally breathe. Even though Dad had said she was safe earlier, it was hard to stop worrying.

"How is she?" I asked.

"Safe but exhausted." Dad paused, choosing his words carefully. "She's seen a lot of really sad, horrible things today."

I looked at him but didn't ask him to explain any further. I'd seen a lot of those things myself.

"She'll be home this evening," Dad added. "Probably late. She's insisting on staying and helping the injured as long as she can."

"And Papa? When will he be home?"

"Probably a few days. He's stuck in Saint Louis, but he said to tell you he's had plenty of time to pick a perfect snow globe for you."

I gave a small smile.

Dad and I both looked across the room at the TV. The news was on, so Dad turned the volume up slightly.

A newscaster explained that a group of terrorists had taken control of several planes and then carried

out the attacks on the United States. Along with the two passenger jets that had crashed into the World Trade Center, another had hit the Pentagon in Washington, D.C. A fourth plane had crashed into a field in Pennsylvania.

When they started showing the footage of the World Trade Center on fire, then crumbling to the ground, Dad turned the TV off.

I was grateful. I didn't need to replay what I'd watched happen in real life.

Dad didn't have to explain to me that a lot of people had died today. My heart hurt for them and their families. I didn't think it would stop hurting anytime soon.

"How could anyone do something so horrible?" I asked my dad. "*Why?*"

It took Dad a moment to answer. "There are people in the world who believe that violence, hurting others, is how they'll get what they want."

"Will they?" I asked.

"No." He shook his head. "Because for every person who wants to cause harm, there are thousands more who want to protect. To do good."

I wanted to believe him. But I also knew things had changed today. Outside our small Manhattan apartment, the smell of smoke still stained the air. Sirens still blared.

I was different. The world was different.

And I wasn't sure things would ever be the same.

CHAPTER TEN

The last time Dad talked to Gran, she'd explained that her station would be taking shifts all night. She was set to come home this morning, but with phone service still mostly down, we weren't sure exactly when. Papa wouldn't be home until tomorrow, when planes would be allowed to fly again.

"Here's another one," Adi sing-songed. She handed me what had to be the twentieth paper chain she'd made.

We wanted to give Gran a hero's welcome, so we'd gathered all the construction paper and leftover birthday decorations. The living room looked like a mismatched party shop. A taped-together paper banner that my sister and I had decorated read, *We Love You, Gran!*

It was a mess, but Gran would love it.

Adi and I sat at the front window, waiting and watching. From the third floor, the city was almost unrecognizable. Everything outside was still coated in ash. Even more roads were now blocked off.

Smoke still rose into the sky from Ground Zero – the place where the towers had collapsed. The sounds of construction equipment could be heard at all hours. Large, bright lights lit up the area after dark so emergency responders could continue searching for survivors.

A tall, metal fence was going up too. It would help keep people out of danger and allow emergency responders to clean up the area near the attacks. The fence would cut our neighbourhood in half.

We were on the "safe" side – out of the Frozen Zone. We wouldn't have to evacuate if we didn't want to.

"Oh!" Adi gasped. "There she is!" She jumped up and pointed at the street, where Gran was walking from the nearest bus stop. "Gran's home! Dad – Gran's home!"

"I heard you," Dad said, coming into the room. "Remember, Gran is really tired. Let's keep it calm, okay?" He raised an eyebrow in Adi's direction.

She gave an exaggerated nod.

When Gran walked through the door, Adi managed to keep her cool. She walked up to Gran and gave her a hug, then handed her the bouquet of flowers she'd gathered from our small balcony garden. She'd had to brush some ash off the petals.

"Hi, Gran," I said. "We missed you."

"Oh, I missed you all too." Gran released a long breath. "More than you know."

She put her bag down and made her way into the living room. It was our same Gran, but she seemed different. She walked slowly, minus her usual pep.

"Adi–" Dad said, looking at my sister and nodding towards the kitchen door.

"Right," Adi said. She went to get the cookies we'd made for Gran early that morning.

Gran sat down on the sofa, and I sat next to her but not too close. Dad had reminded us to give her space.

Just then a loud crash came from the kitchen. The noise made Gran's shoulders jump.

"Oops!" Adi said from the other room.

"I'm on it. . . ." Dad rushed to the kitchen.

Gran stared at her lap, then up at me. Her eyes were red around the edges. I couldn't tell if she'd been crying or was tired – probably both.

"I'm so glad you're safe," I said. "I was really worried."

I felt the tears forming and tried to hold them back. I didn't want to make her sadder than she already seemed.

Gran scooted closer and put her arm around me. Her signature perfume – lavender and mint – hit me. It was instantly calming.

"It's been a rough couple of days," she said. "And it's only going to get harder. But I'm here. We're all here. And we're safe." She looked into my eyes and smiled. "I was very worried about you and your sister too."

I looked across at her and smiled back. A moment later, the kitchen door swung open. Dad and Adi entered the living room with a plate of cookies and a cup of tea.

My sister sat on Gran's other side and hugged her. "Are you happy to be home, Gran?" she asked.

Gran sipped her tea. "So very happy," she said, giving Adi a squeeze. But she didn't seem happy. Not truly. Still, she smiled. "Now, let me try one of these cookies."

Molly's apartment
Tribeca, New York City
13 September 2001

Papa returned home the next afternoon. The airport must have had a decent souvenir selection because he brought me my favourite snow globe yet – a large glass dome with the Saint Louis Arch inside. Each time I turned it over, the tiny elevator went up and over the arch.

After a good night's sleep, Gran seemed more herself. She decided to return to work. She didn't have to go back so soon, but she wanted to volunteer.

I was proud of her but worried. The danger wasn't over. I'd overheard Dad and Papa watching the news. They were discussing toxic fumes down at Ground Zero, the possibility of wreckage collapsing.

That evening, as Gran was putting on her uniform jacket, I stopped her. "Are you worried about going back? I heard it's still dangerous."

Gran nodded. "Of course I'm worried. But it's what I need to do. Our hardest work is only beginning."

Molly's apartment
Tribeca, New York City
12 March 2002

Six months later, we were finally home. Because we lived so close to Ground Zero, Dad, Papa and Gran had agreed it was best to leave our neighbourhood for a while. The smoke and strong chemical smells hadn't cleared as quickly as we hoped. Fires had burned at the World Trade Center site for three months after the attacks.

Adi and I had transferred to another school. We'd got a temporary lease on a different apartment. It was far enough from where the Twin Towers had fallen that we wouldn't be breathing in dust and ash as workers continued to clean up the wreckage.

We'd still been close enough for Gran to volunteer at her station in the weeks following the attacks. But I had to admit, it had been nice not seeing Ground Zero out of my window every morning. I hadn't wanted the reminder. There were already too many.

We went to the doctor a lot to make sure we were all healthy – especially Gran, Adi and me, since we'd been so close to the towers when they fell. We were all healthy. Gran had some long-lasting bronchitis, but the doctors said she was lucky.

We started seeing a therapist too. I was waking

up in the middle of the night and could feel the heat sizzling off the buildings. I had nightmares about being lost in the city, looking for Adi, everything covered in ash and dust. . . . I saw those towers fall in the back of my mind a lot, even though I tried not to think about it.

Gran struggled too, though she didn't talk about it much. When there was a loud noise, she jumped. If something about the attacks came on TV, she immediately tensed and left the room.

The therapist explained that we all had some form of post-traumatic stress disorder – PTSD.

One thing that helped Gran was an organization that brought therapy dogs to her station. The dogs helped boost the spirits of firefighters and EMTs and other first responders. People who, like Gran, worked long, exhausting hours in the days after the attacks.

A lot of those people lost friends and family. Several of the men and women Gran worked with were injured badly. Some died.

That's part of the reason why Gran decided to take a step back from work after things started to calm down. She took a temporary leave of absence.

Dad and Papa said she eventually wanted to return to her job as an EMT. But it would take time. And it was okay if she decided not to return at all.

On our first night back in our own apartment, Gran read our story. We went back to how it used to be when Adi and I were small. We all piled into Dad and Papa's big bed.

"*The Frog King,*" Gran said, settling back into the pillows.

She opened the book to the first page of the story. "In old times, when wishing still helped one, there lived a king whose daughters were all beautiful, but the youngest was so beautiful that the sun itself, which has seen so much, was

astonished whenever it shone in her face . . ."

I stared out of the window and listened to Gran's voice. From the bed, I could see the gigantic blue lights that indicated where the World Trade Center had stood.

Two tall, brilliant blue pillars glowed like the Twin Towers' spirits. As if they still watched over us, beacons guiding us home.

A NOTE FROM
THE AUTHOR

As an author whose main genre is fantasy, it was both a welcome challenge and a great honour to write Molly's story. At the point of this writing, the terrorist attacks of September 11, 2001, are the most modern historical topic explored within the Girls Survive series. With that fact comes great responsibility. The events of that day – and the estimated 2,606 lives lost – are still very fresh in the hearts and minds of many. Having lived during the time of the tragedy made writing about it both helpful – because I remember much of that horrible day firsthand – and extremely difficult – because I remember much of that horrible day firsthand.

Despite that, in writing about the events of September 11, 2001, there was still much for me to learn. In researching the World Trade Center, I discovered not only that it was briefly the tallest building in the world, but also that the grandeur of the towers inspired several death-defying stunts. Daredevils of the day attempted stunts ranging from a heart-stopping tightrope walk between the two buildings to scaling the South Tower using a homemade climbing contraption. The draw of the World Trade Center was undeniable.

While the towers were indeed a feat of engineering, it was the people of the World Trade Center – many of whom became heroes that tragic day in September – who truly touched my heart. First responders and volunteers heroically saved twenty-five thousand people from the World Trade Center. There are many stories of individuals who worked in or near the Twin Towers who risked their lives climbing to the top floors to help rescue others.

One such story I found particularly touching is that of Frank De Martini and Pablo Ortiz. Both men worked for the Port Authority and were in the North Tower when American Airlines Flight 11 crashed into the building. Instead of rushing to safety, these two men climbed to the 88th and 89th floors to help people who were trapped near the top of the tower. They cleared the way by forcing open elevator doors and pushing through debris-filled offices. They courageously guided people through the smoke and flames to exits. De Martini and Ortiz are credited with saving up to fifty lives that day.

Another lifesaving volunteer was Sister Cynthia Mahoney, who had moved from South Carolina to New York City shortly before the September 11 attacks occurred. Not only was Sister Cindy a nun, she was also trained as an EMT. She didn't think twice before hopping into an ambulance and volunteering. Sister Cindy spent six months at Ground Zero, counselling those in need as well as helping in the recovery of victims and blessing their remains. She became known as the "Angel of Ground Zero".

It wasn't only people who helped others that day and in the months to follow. I'd heard that there were dogs who assisted at Ground Zero, but I hadn't looked into it until writing this book. I was in awe when I discovered the many canine heroes who worked at Ground Zero.

Dogs were brought in as therapy animals to help comfort those with PTSD and to lift the spirits of the injured. There were also several specially trained dogs and handlers – some of whom travelled from as far away as California – who helped in the rescue and recovery after the attacks.

Two of those dogs were golden retrievers, Bretagne and Riley. Bretagne was just two years old when the attacks occurred. She and her handler worked tirelessly at Ground Zero for ten straight days. Bretagne went on to help in rescue missions during natural disasters. She later retired and became a goodwill ambassador.

Riley was trained specifically in live-rescue and travelled to Ground Zero, where he searched desperately to locate anyone who might still be trapped in the rubble. When those efforts ended, Riley then shifted to help in the recovery and provided comfort to the humans he worked alongside.

In researching Molly's neighbourhood of Tribeca, I also discovered heartwarming stories about neighbours and business owners coming together in their own ways to help with the efforts and aftermath. Many of the people in Tribeca evacuated, but some stayed. And those who did stay opened their restaurants and homes to feed rescue workers, neighbours and first responders.

In writing Molly's story, which was entrenched in so much terror and confusion, I truly tried to keep an underlying sense of hope. I wanted to not only create a relatable story about a young woman – and her sassy little sister – who lived through an incredibly scary tragedy, but to also show how she and her family came out on the other side of it. Maybe not perfectly, maybe not the same as they were before, but together and with hope still intact.

MAKING CONNECTIONS

1. In Chapter Four, Molly decides to stray from fellow pupils and teachers to go and find her sister. Do you think Molly made the right choice in leaving the group? Do you think it was a safe choice? Is Zach a good friend for going with her, or should he have tried harder to talk her into staying? Explain your answer.

2. Living in one of the busiest cities in the world plays a big role in the story and in Molly's survival. How do you think the tragedy of 11 September 2001, would have been different had it occurred in a less populated location? How would a different setting have affected Molly, Zach and Adi's escape?

3. Throughout the book, Adi finds comfort in their family cat, Rolo. After the attacks, Gran finds comfort in the therapy dogs that visit her fire station. Recall a time when a pet comforted you during a difficult moment, and write a few sentences about your experience. What benefits might therapy animals provide?

GLOSSARY

anonymously written, done or given by a person whose name is not known or made public

bronchitis illness of the throat and lungs

chaotic state of complete confusion and disorder

commotion noisy excitement and confusion

debris scattered pieces of something that has been broken or destroyed

EMT person trained to give emergency medical care to a patient before and on the way to a hospital

engulfed flow over and cover or surround

evacuate leave a dangerous place to go somewhere safer

foreign out of place or unfamiliar

haze fine dust, smoke or fine particles or water in the air that make it hard to see clearly

hijack take control of an aircraft or other vehicle by force

lease rent property or resources for a period of time

leave of absence period of time when someone has special permission to be away from a job

maintenance upkeep

plea serious and emotional request for something

rambunctious not under control, in a way that is playful or full of energy

retire give up work, usually because of a person's age

sexist unfair treatment of a person because of his or her gender

silhouette outline of something that shows its shape

speculate come up with ideas or theories about something

surrogate person who takes the place or performs the duties of someone or something else, such as carrying a child

toxic poisonous

ABOUT THE AUTHOR

Jessika Fleck is a writer, unapologetic coffee drinker and knitter who sincerely hopes to one day discover a way to do all three at once. Until then, she continues collecting vintage typewriters and hourglasses, dreaming of an Ireland getaway and convincing her husband they NEED more kittens. She has lived all over the United States, from Hawaii to Vermont, but currently lives in Illinois, where she's learning to appreciate the beauty in cornfields and terrifyingly large cicadas. She lives there with her sociology professor husband and two daughters.